DOWNERS GROVE PUBLIC LIBRARY

3 1191 00944 5

NOV 1 1 2010

W9-BNN-511

JUNIOR ROOM
DOWNERS GROVE PUBLIC LIBRARY

WITHDRAWN DOWNERS GROVE PUBLIC LIBRARY

J/COMIC WOLVERINE
Van Lente, Fred.
The buddy system

Downers Grove Public Library

1050 Curtiss St.

Downers Grove, IL 60515

(630) 960-1200

www.downersgrovelibrary.org

GAYLORD

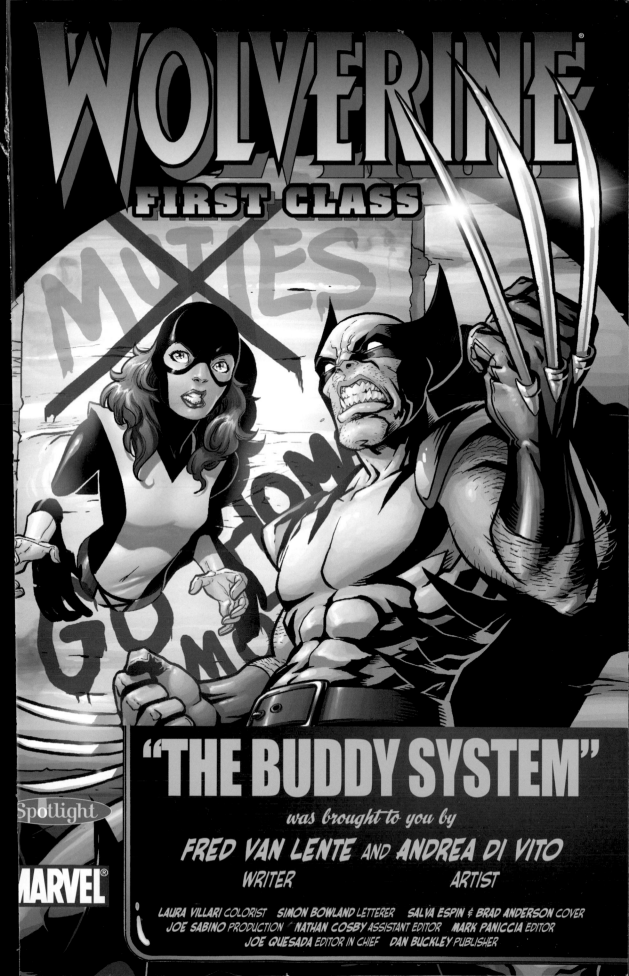

WOLVERINE
FIRST CLASS

"THE BUDDY SYSTEM"

was brought to you by

FRED VAN LENTE AND ANDREA DI VITO
WRITER · ARTIST

LAURA VILLARI COLORIST · SIMON BOWLAND LETTERER · SALVA ESPIN & BRAD ANDERSON COVER

JOE SABINO PRODUCTION · NATHAN COSBY ASSISTANT EDITOR · MARK PANICCIA EDITOR

JOE QUESADA EDITOR IN CHIEF · DAN BUCKLEY PUBLISHER

Spotlight

MARVEL®

VISIT US AT
www.abdopublishing.com

Reinforced library bound edition published in 2010 by Spotlight, a division of the ABDO Group, 8000 West 78th Street, Edina, Minnesota 55439. Spotlight produces high-quality reinforced library bound editions for schools and libraries. Published by agreement with Marvel Characters, Inc.

Copyright © 2009 Marvel Entertainment, Inc. and its subsidiaries. MARVEL, all related characters and the distinctive likenesses thereof are trademarks of Marvel Entertainment, Inc. and its subsidiaries, and are used with permissions. Copyright © 2009 Marvel Entertainment, Inc. and its subsidiaries. Licensed by Marvel Characters B.V. www.marvel.com, All rights reserved.

MARVEL, Wolverine: TM & © 2009 Marvel Characters, Inc. All rights reserved. www.marvel.com. This book is produced under license from Marvel Characters, Inc.

Library of Congress Cataloging-in-Publication Data

Van Lente, Fred.
  The buddy system / Fred Van Lente, writer ; Andrea Di Vito, artist ; Laura Villari, colorist ; Simon Bowland, letterer. -- Reinforced library bound ed.
     p. cm. -- (Wolverine, first class)
  "Marvel."
  ISBN 978-1-59961-669-8
  1. Graphic novels. 2. Graphic novels. [1. Graphic novels. 2. Superheroes--Fiction.] I. Di Vito, Andrea, ill. II. Villari, Laura. III. Bowland, Simon. IV. Title.
  PZ7.7.V26Bu 2010
  741.5'973--dc22
                              2009010134

All Spotlight books have reinforced library bindings and are manufactured in the United States of

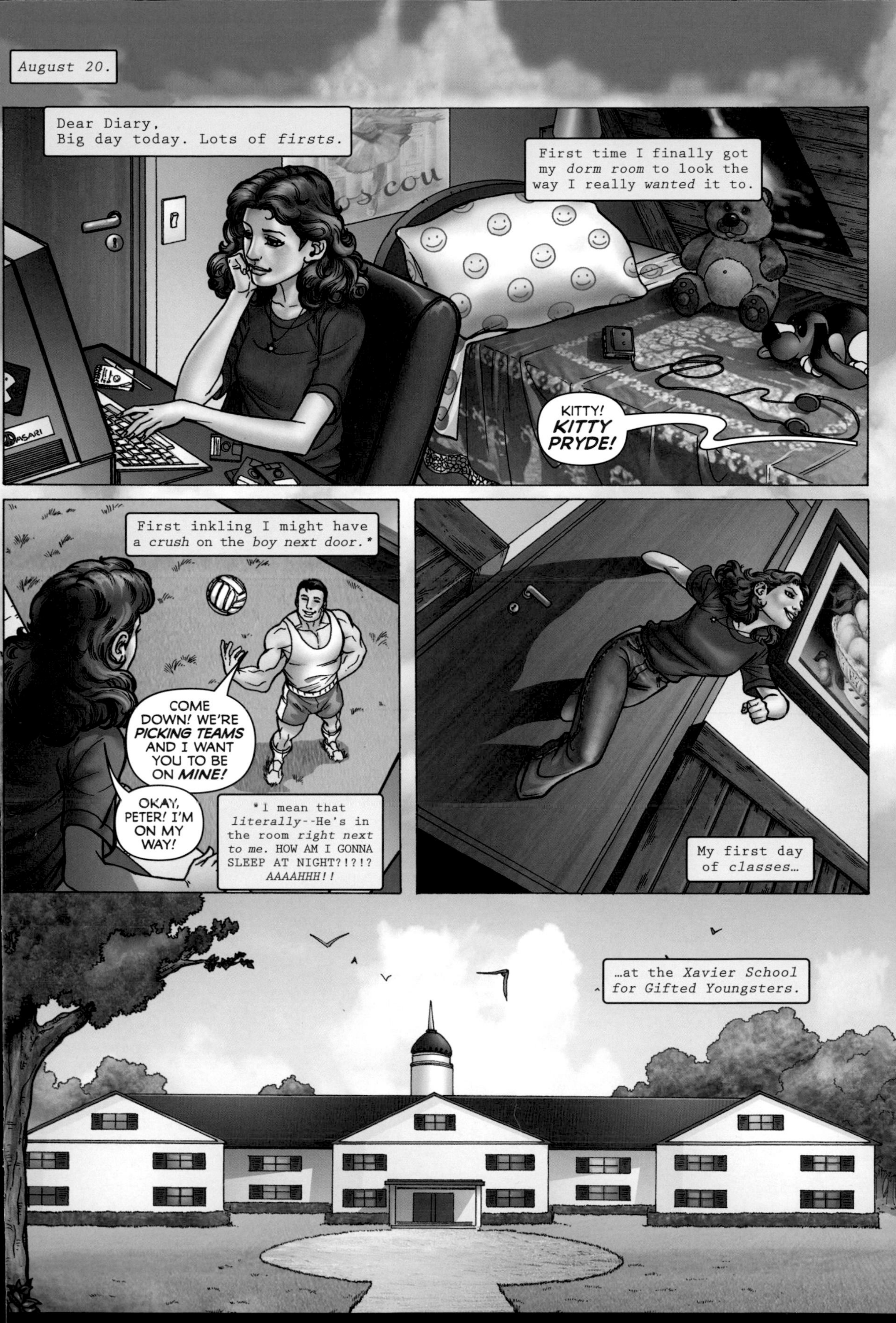
August 20.
Dear Diary,
Big day today. Lots of *firsts*.
First time I finally got my *dorm room* to look the way I really *wanted* it to.
KITTY! ***KITTY PRYDE!***
First inkling I might have a *crush* on the *boy next door*.*
COME DOWN! WE'RE ***PICKING TEAMS*** AND I WANT YOU TO BE ON ***MINE!***
OKAY, PETER! I'M ON MY WAY!
*I mean that *literally*--He's in the room *right next to me*. HOW AM I GONNA SLEEP AT NIGHT?!?!? *AAAAHHH!!*
My first day of *classes*…
…at the *Xavier School for Gifted Youngsters*.

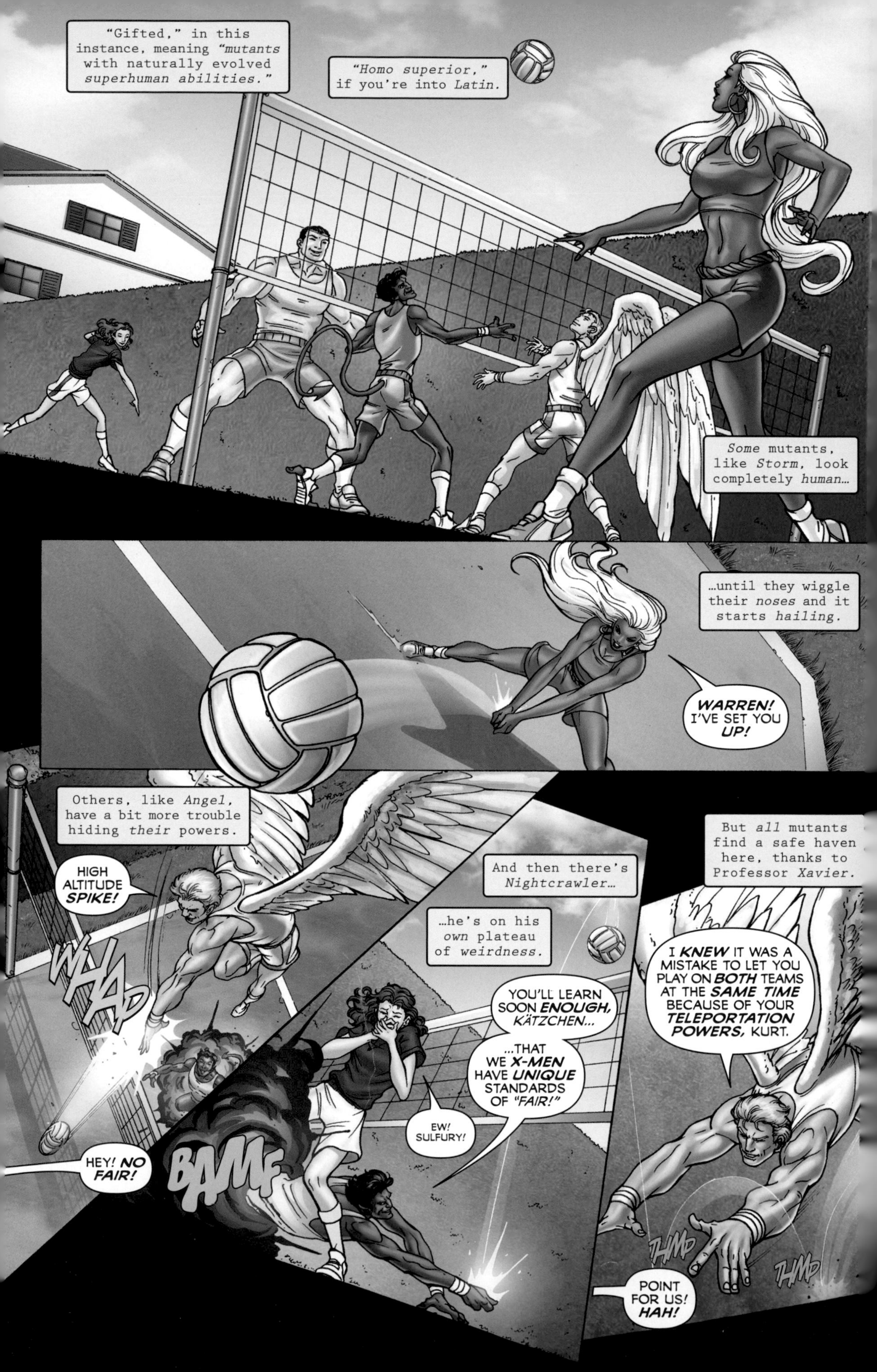
"Gifted," in this instance, meaning "mutants with naturally evolved superhuman abilities."
"Homo superior," if you're into Latin.
Some mutants, like Storm, look completely human...
...until they wiggle their noses and it starts hailing.
WARREN! I'VE SET YOU UP!
Others, like Angel, have a bit more trouble hiding their powers.
HIGH ALTITUDE SPIKE!
WHAP
HEY! NO FAIR!
And then there's Nightcrawler...
...he's on his own plateau of weirdness.
YOU'LL LEARN SOON ENOUGH, KÄTZCHEN...
...THAT WE X-MEN HAVE UNIQUE STANDARDS OF "FAIR!"
EW! SULFURY!
BAMF
But all mutants find a safe haven here, thanks to Professor Xavier.
I KNEW IT WAS A MISTAKE TO LET YOU PLAY ON BOTH TEAMS AT THE SAME TIME BECAUSE OF YOUR TELEPORTATION POWERS, KURT.
THMP
THMP
POINT FOR US! HAH!

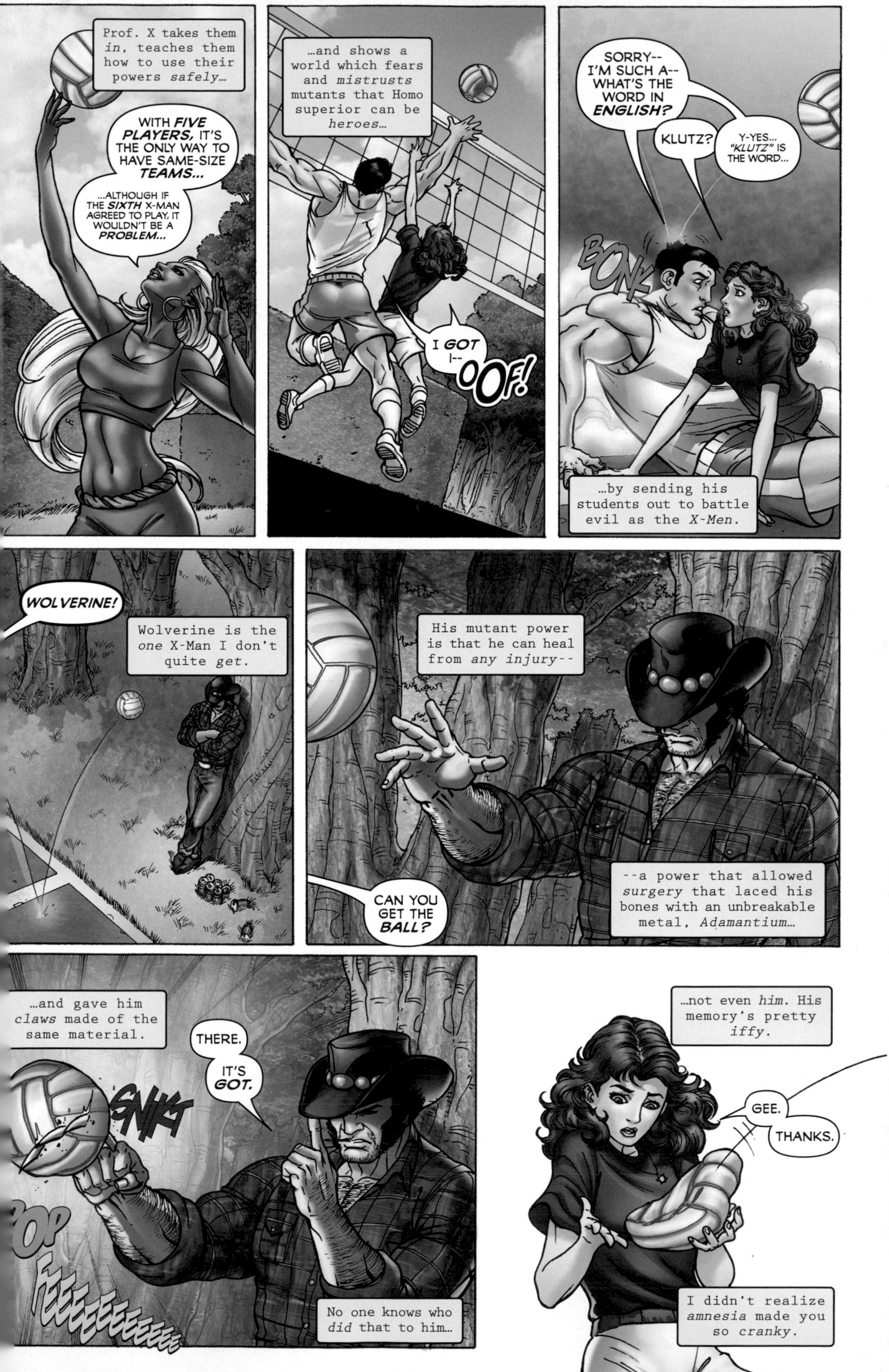
Prof. X takes them *in*, teaches them how to use their powers *safely*...
WITH ***FIVE PLAYERS,*** IT'S THE ONLY WAY TO HAVE SAME-SIZE ***TEAMS...***
...ALTHOUGH IF THE ***SIXTH*** X-MAN AGREED TO PLAY, IT WOULDN'T BE A ***PROBLEM...***
...and shows a world which fears and *mistrusts* mutants that Homo superior can be *heroes*...
I ***GOT*** I--
OOF!
SORRY-- I'M SUCH A-- WHAT'S THE WORD IN ***ENGLISH?***
KLUTZ?
Y-YES... *"KLUTZ"* IS THE WORD...
BONK
...by sending his students out to battle evil as the *X-Men.*
WOLVERINE!
Wolverine is the *one* X-Man I don't quite *get.*
His mutant power is that he can heal from *any injury*--
CAN YOU GET THE ***BALL?***
--a power that allowed *surgery* that laced his bones with an unbreakable metal, *Adamantium*...
...and gave him *claws* made of the same material.
THERE.
IT'S ***GOT.***
SNIKT
POP
FEEEEEEEEEEE
No one knows who *did* that to him...
...not even *him.* His memory's pretty *iffy.*
GEE.
THANKS.
I didn't realize *amnesia* made you so *cranky.*

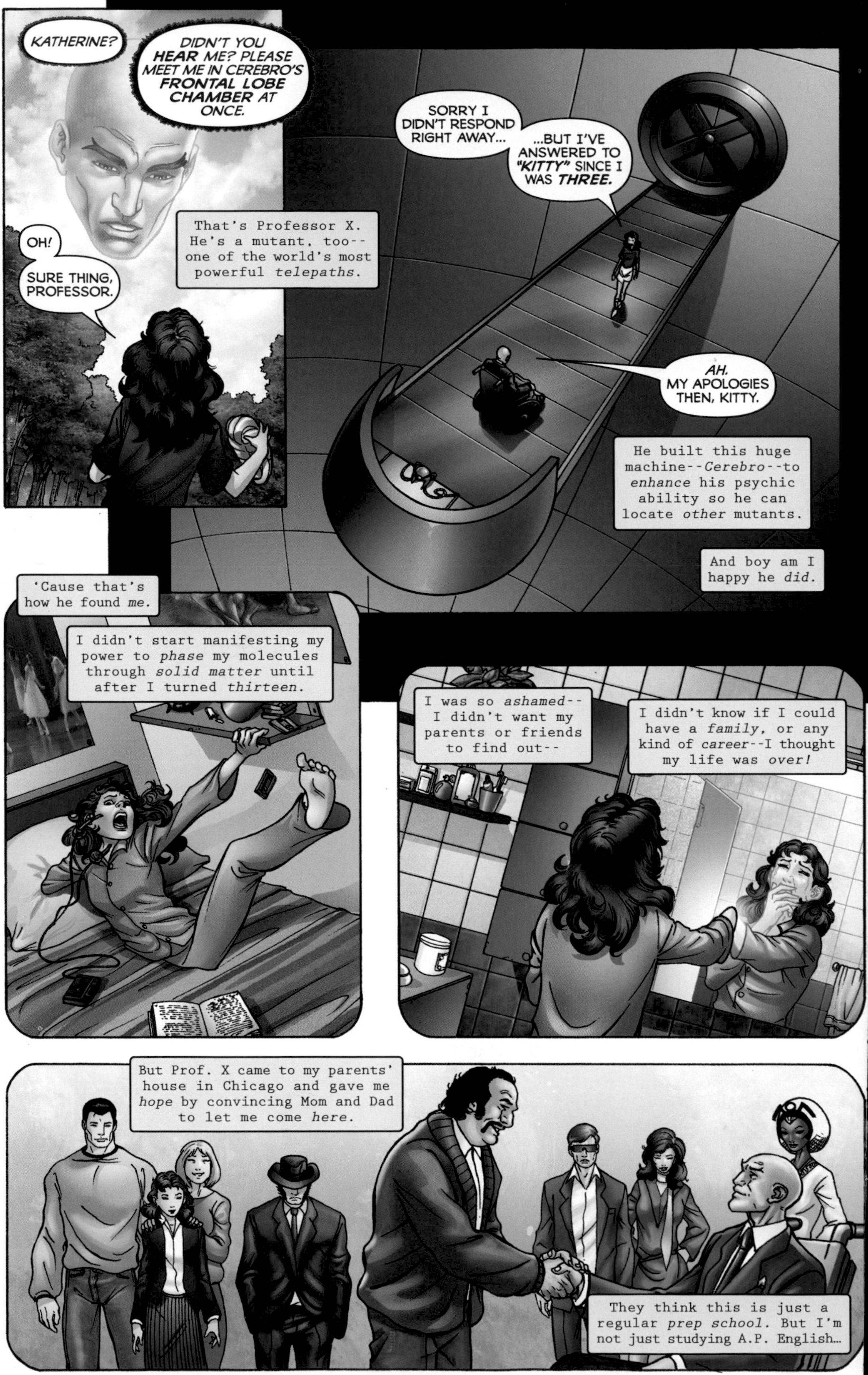

KATHERINE?
DIDN'T YOU HEAR ME? PLEASE MEET ME IN CEREBRO'S FRONTAL LOBE CHAMBER AT ONCE.
OH!
SURE THING, PROFESSOR.
That's Professor X. He's a mutant, too--one of the world's most powerful telepaths.
SORRY I DIDN'T RESPOND RIGHT AWAY...
...BUT I'VE ANSWERED TO "KITTY" SINCE I WAS THREE.
AH. MY APOLOGIES THEN, KITTY.
He built this huge machine--Cerebro--to enhance his psychic ability so he can locate other mutants.
And boy am I happy he did.
'Cause that's how he found me.
I didn't start manifesting my power to phase my molecules through solid matter until after I turned thirteen.
I was so ashamed--I didn't want my parents or friends to find out--
I didn't know if I could have a family, or any kind of career--I thought my life was over!
But Prof. X came to my parents' house in Chicago and gave me hope by convincing Mom and Dad to let me come here.
They think this is just a regular prep school. But I'm not just studying A.P. English...

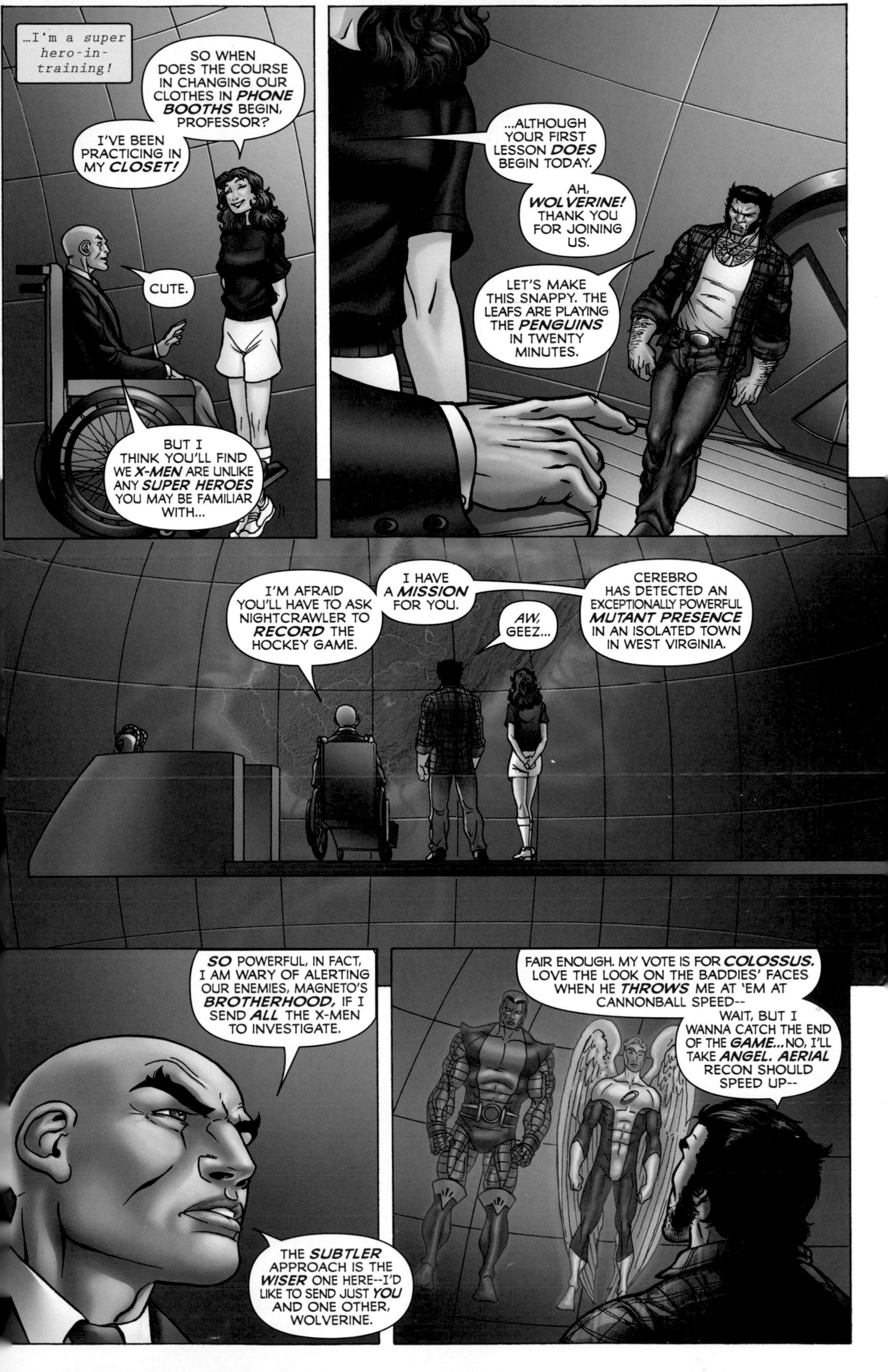
...I'm a super hero-in-training!
SO WHEN DOES THE COURSE IN CHANGING OUR CLOTHES IN PHONE BOOTHS BEGIN, PROFESSOR?
I'VE BEEN PRACTICING IN MY CLOSET!
CUTE.
BUT I THINK YOU'LL FIND WE X-MEN ARE UNLIKE ANY SUPER HEROES YOU MAY BE FAMILIAR WITH...
...ALTHOUGH YOUR FIRST LESSON DOES BEGIN TODAY.
AH, WOLVERINE! THANK YOU FOR JOINING US.
LET'S MAKE THIS SNAPPY. THE LEAFS ARE PLAYING THE PENGUINS IN TWENTY MINUTES.
I'M AFRAID YOU'LL HAVE TO ASK NIGHTCRAWLER TO RECORD THE HOCKEY GAME.
I HAVE A MISSION FOR YOU.
CEREBRO HAS DETECTED AN EXCEPTIONALLY POWERFUL MUTANT PRESENCE IN AN ISOLATED TOWN IN WEST VIRGINIA.
AW, GEEZ...
SO POWERFUL, IN FACT, I AM WARY OF ALERTING OUR ENEMIES, MAGNETO'S BROTHERHOOD, IF I SEND ALL THE X-MEN TO INVESTIGATE.
THE SUBTLER APPROACH IS THE WISER ONE HERE--I'D LIKE TO SEND JUST YOU AND ONE OTHER, WOLVERINE.
FAIR ENOUGH. MY VOTE IS FOR COLOSSUS. LOVE THE LOOK ON THE BADDIES' FACES WHEN HE THROWS ME AT 'EM AT CANNONBALL SPEED--
WAIT, BUT I WANNA CATCH THE END OF THE GAME...NO, I'LL TAKE ANGEL. AERIAL RECON SHOULD SPEED UP--

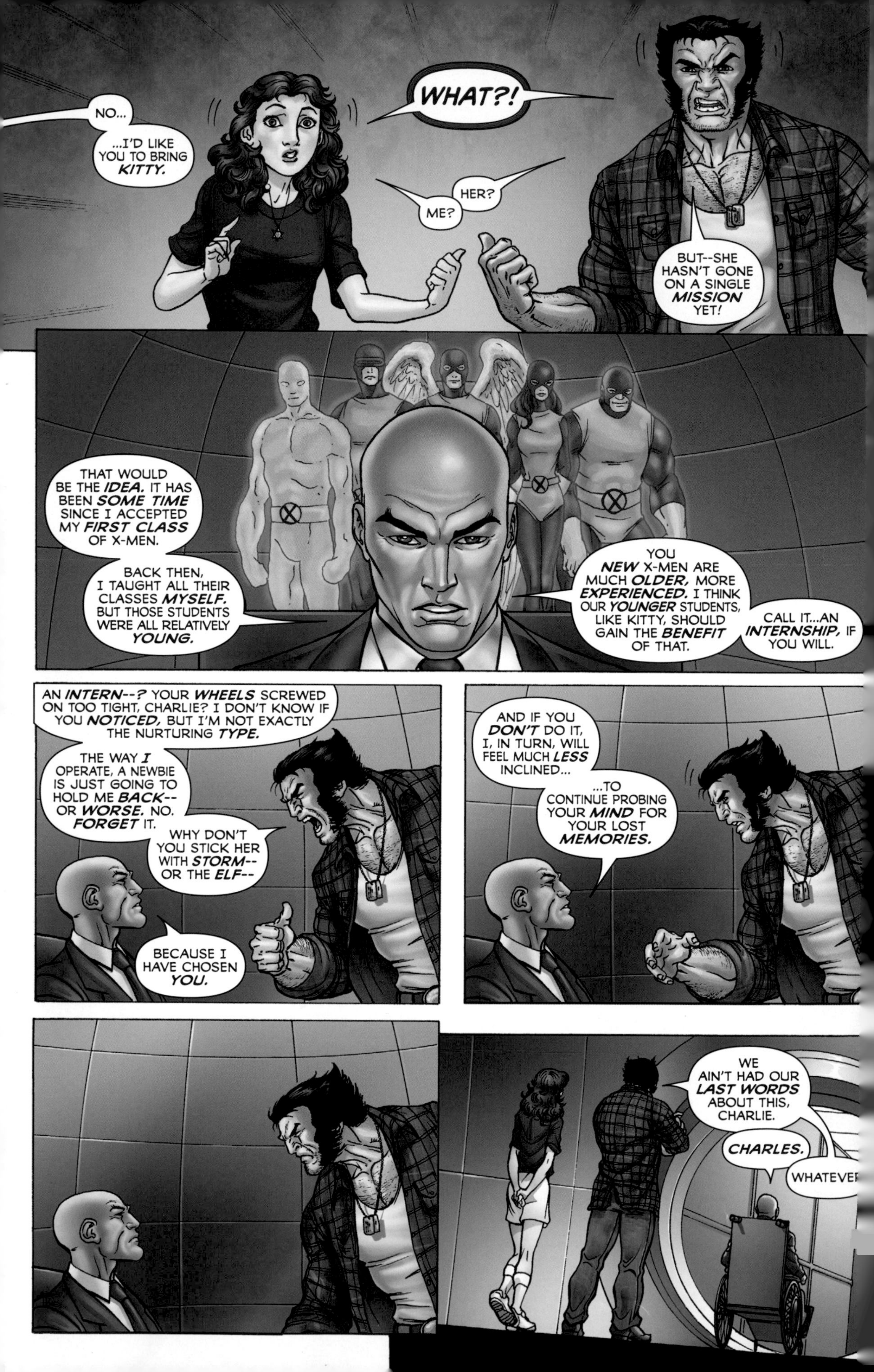
NO...
...I'D LIKE YOU TO BRING KITTY.
WHAT?!
ME?
HER?
BUT--SHE HASN'T GONE ON A SINGLE MISSION YET!
THAT WOULD BE THE IDEA. IT HAS BEEN SOME TIME SINCE I ACCEPTED MY FIRST CLASS OF X-MEN.
BACK THEN, I TAUGHT ALL THEIR CLASSES MYSELF. BUT THOSE STUDENTS WERE ALL RELATIVELY YOUNG.
YOU NEW X-MEN ARE MUCH OLDER, MORE EXPERIENCED. I THINK OUR YOUNGER STUDENTS, LIKE KITTY, SHOULD GAIN THE BENEFIT OF THAT.
CALL IT...AN INTERNSHIP, IF YOU WILL.
AN INTERN--? YOUR WHEELS SCREWED ON TOO TIGHT, CHARLIE? I DON'T KNOW IF YOU NOTICED, BUT I'M NOT EXACTLY THE NURTURING TYPE.
THE WAY I OPERATE, A NEWBIE IS JUST GOING TO HOLD ME BACK-- OR WORSE. NO. FORGET IT.
WHY DON'T YOU STICK HER WITH STORM-- OR THE ELF--
BECAUSE I HAVE CHOSEN YOU.
AND IF YOU DON'T DO IT, I, IN TURN, WILL FEEL MUCH LESS INCLINED...
...TO CONTINUE PROBING YOUR MIND FOR YOUR LOST MEMORIES.
WE AIN'T HAD OUR LAST WORDS ABOUT THIS, CHARLIE.
CHARLES.
WHATEVER

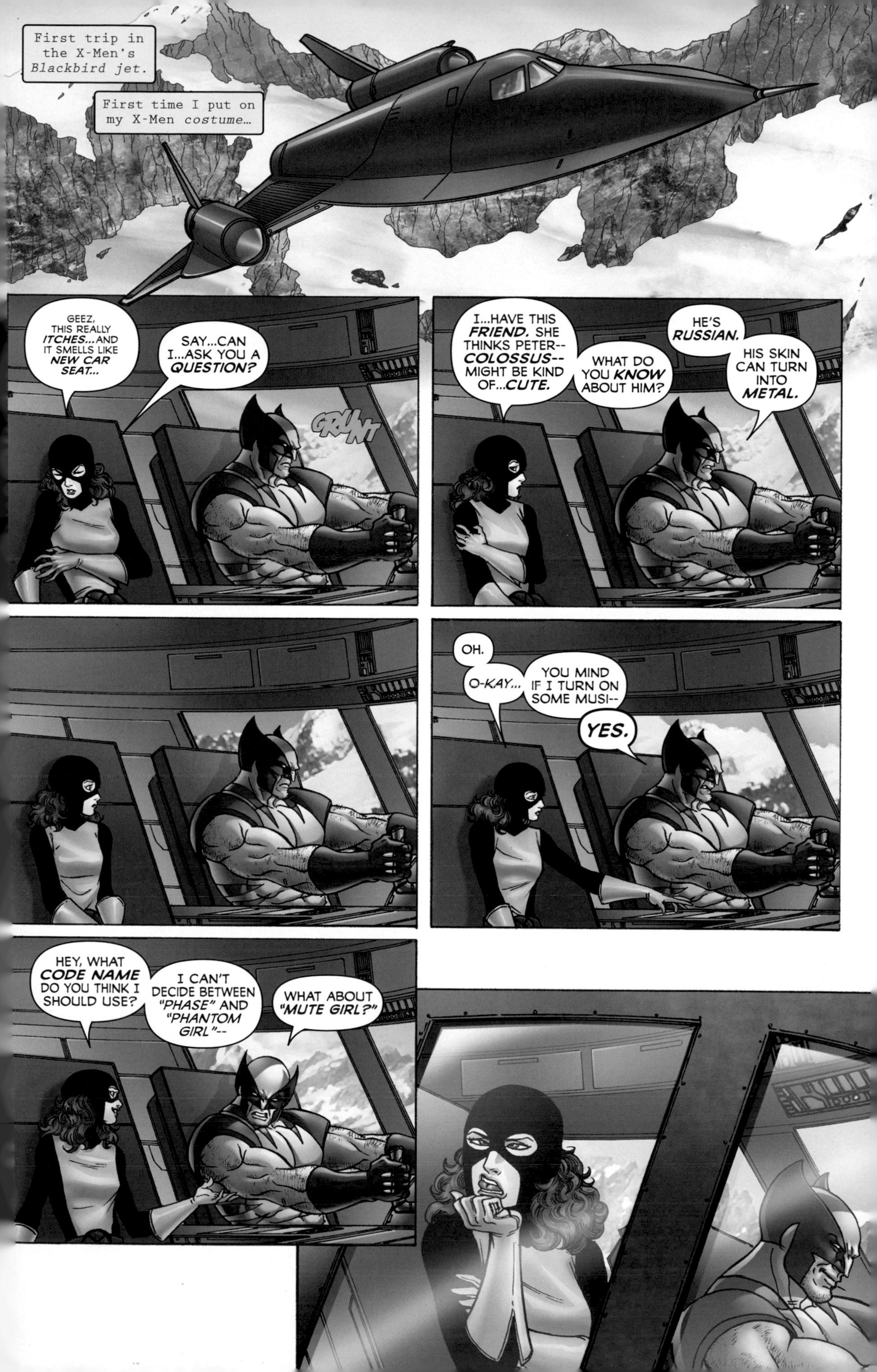
First trip in the X-Men's *Blackbird jet.*
First time I put on my X-Men *costume...*
GEEZ, THIS REALLY *ITCHES*... AND IT SMELLS LIKE *NEW CAR SEAT*...
SAY...CAN I...ASK YOU A *QUESTION?*
GRUNT
I...HAVE THIS *FRIEND.* SHE THINKS PETER-- *COLOSSUS*-- MIGHT BE KIND OF...*CUTE.*
WHAT DO YOU *KNOW* ABOUT HIM?
HE'S *RUSSIAN.*
HIS SKIN CAN TURN INTO *METAL.*
OH.
O-KAY...
YOU MIND IF I TURN ON SOME MUSI--
YES.
HEY, WHAT *CODE NAME* DO YOU THINK I SHOULD USE?
I CAN'T DECIDE BETWEEN "PHASE" AND "PHANTOM GIRL"--
WHAT ABOUT *"MUTE GIRL?"*

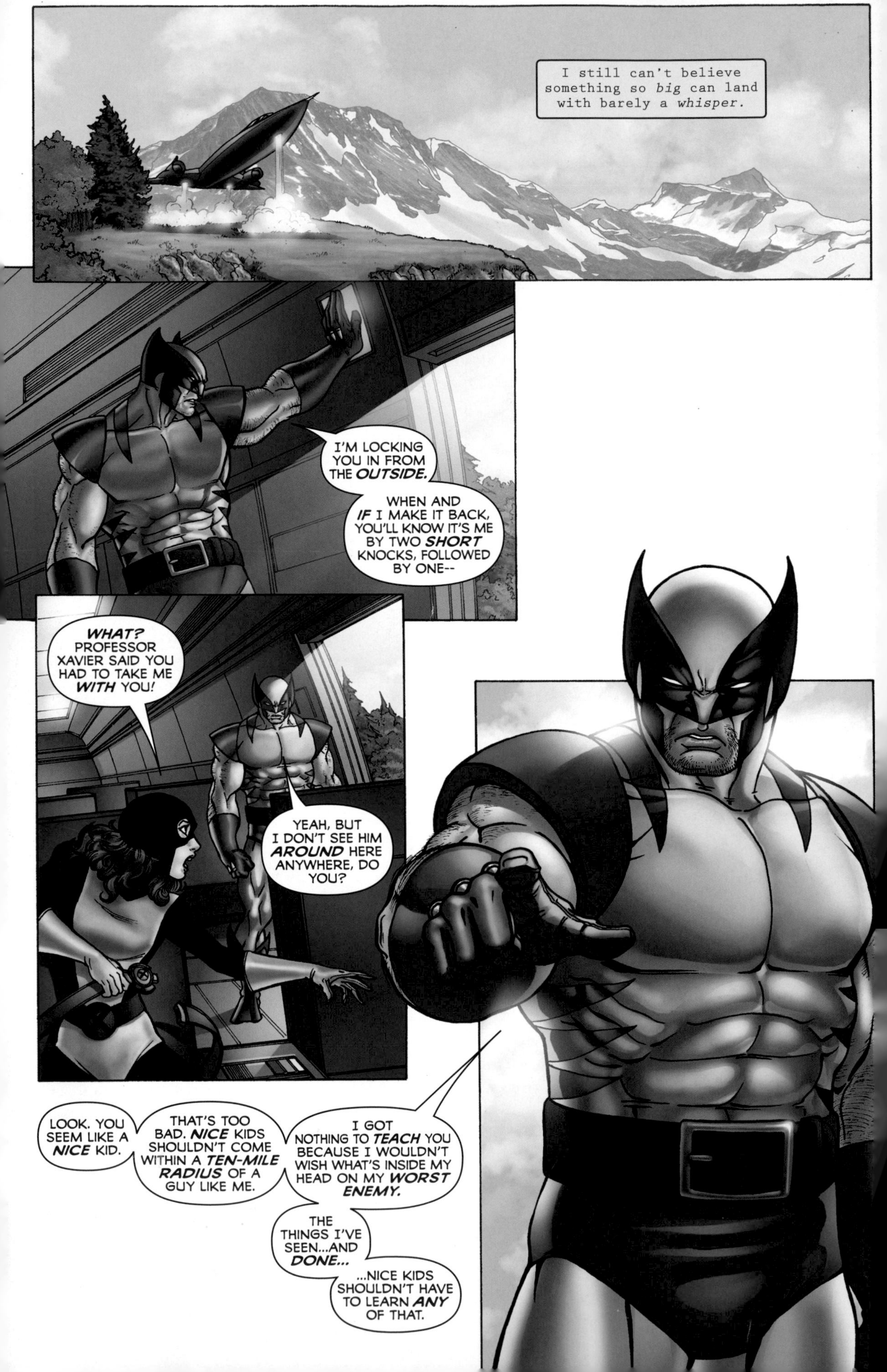

I still can't believe something so *big* can land with barely a *whisper.*
I'M LOCKING YOU IN FROM THE ***OUTSIDE.***
WHEN AND ***IF*** I MAKE IT BACK, YOU'LL KNOW IT'S ME BY TWO ***SHORT*** KNOCKS, FOLLOWED BY ONE--
WHAT? PROFESSOR XAVIER SAID YOU HAD TO TAKE ME ***WITH*** YOU!
YEAH, BUT I DON'T SEE HIM ***AROUND*** HERE ANYWHERE, DO YOU?
LOOK. YOU SEEM LIKE A ***NICE*** KID.
THAT'S TOO BAD. ***NICE*** KIDS SHOULDN'T COME WITHIN A ***TEN-MILE RADIUS*** OF A GUY LIKE ME.
I GOT NOTHING TO ***TEACH*** YOU BECAUSE I WOULDN'T WISH WHAT'S INSIDE MY HEAD ON MY ***WORST ENEMY.***
THE THINGS I'VE SEEN...AND ***DONE...***
...NICE KIDS SHOULDN'T HAVE TO LEARN ***ANY*** OF THAT.

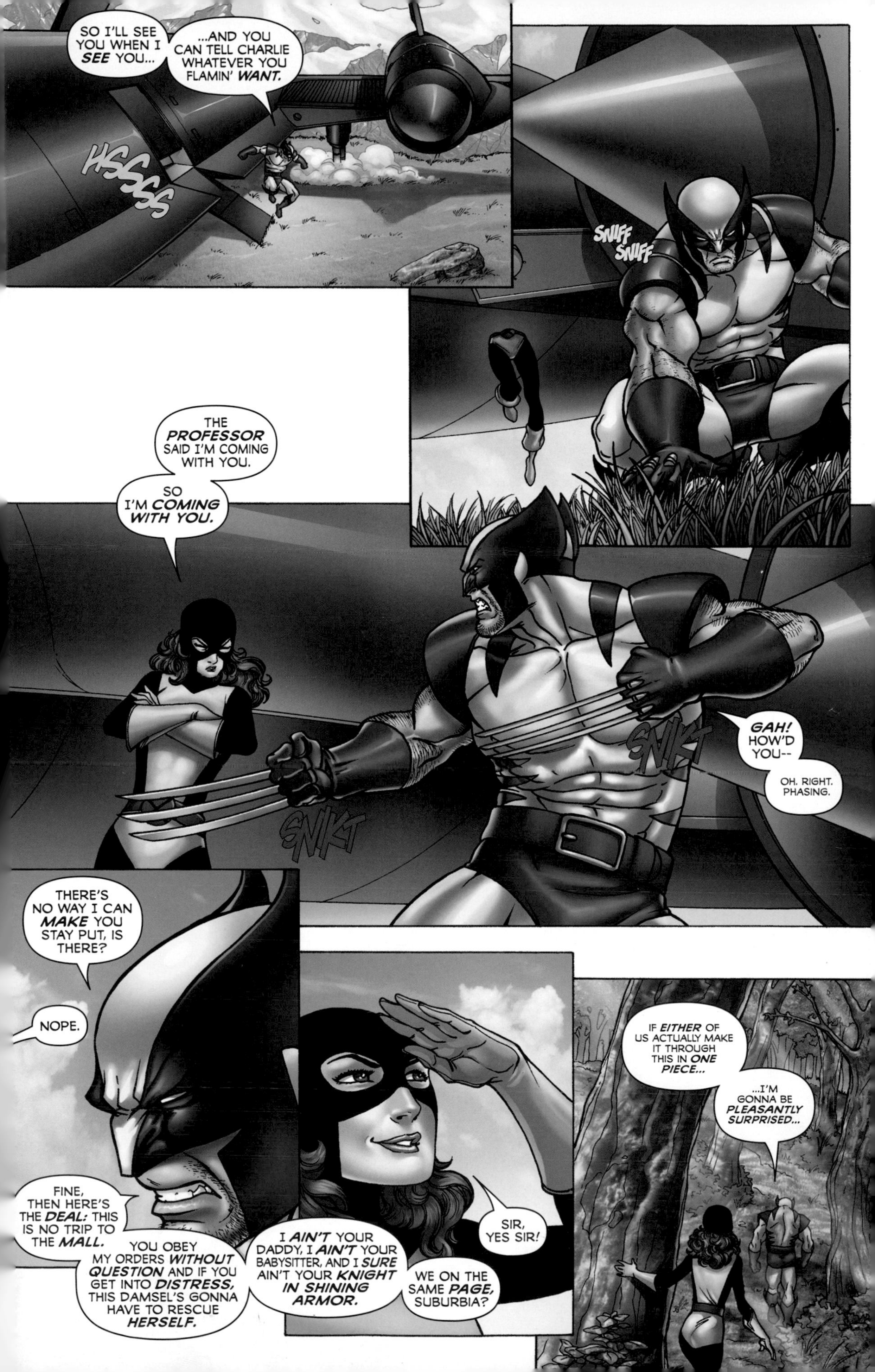

SO I'LL SEE YOU WHEN I SEE YOU...
...AND YOU CAN TELL CHARLIE WHATEVER YOU FLAMIN' WANT.
HSSSSS
SNIFF SNIFF
THE PROFESSOR SAID I'M COMING WITH YOU.
SO I'M COMING WITH YOU.
SNIKT
SNIKT
GAH! HOW'D YOU--
OH. RIGHT. PHASING.
THERE'S NO WAY I CAN MAKE YOU STAY PUT, IS THERE?
NOPE.
FINE, THEN HERE'S THE DEAL: THIS IS NO TRIP TO THE MALL.
YOU OBEY MY ORDERS WITHOUT QUESTION AND IF YOU GET INTO DISTRESS, THIS DAMSEL'S GONNA HAVE TO RESCUE HERSELF.
I AIN'T YOUR DADDY, I AIN'T YOUR BABYSITTER, AND I SURE AIN'T YOUR KNIGHT IN SHINING ARMOR.
WE ON THE SAME PAGE, SUBURBIA?
SIR, YES SIR!
IF EITHER OF US ACTUALLY MAKE IT THROUGH THIS IN ONE PIECE...
...I'M GONNA BE PLEASANTLY SURPRISED...

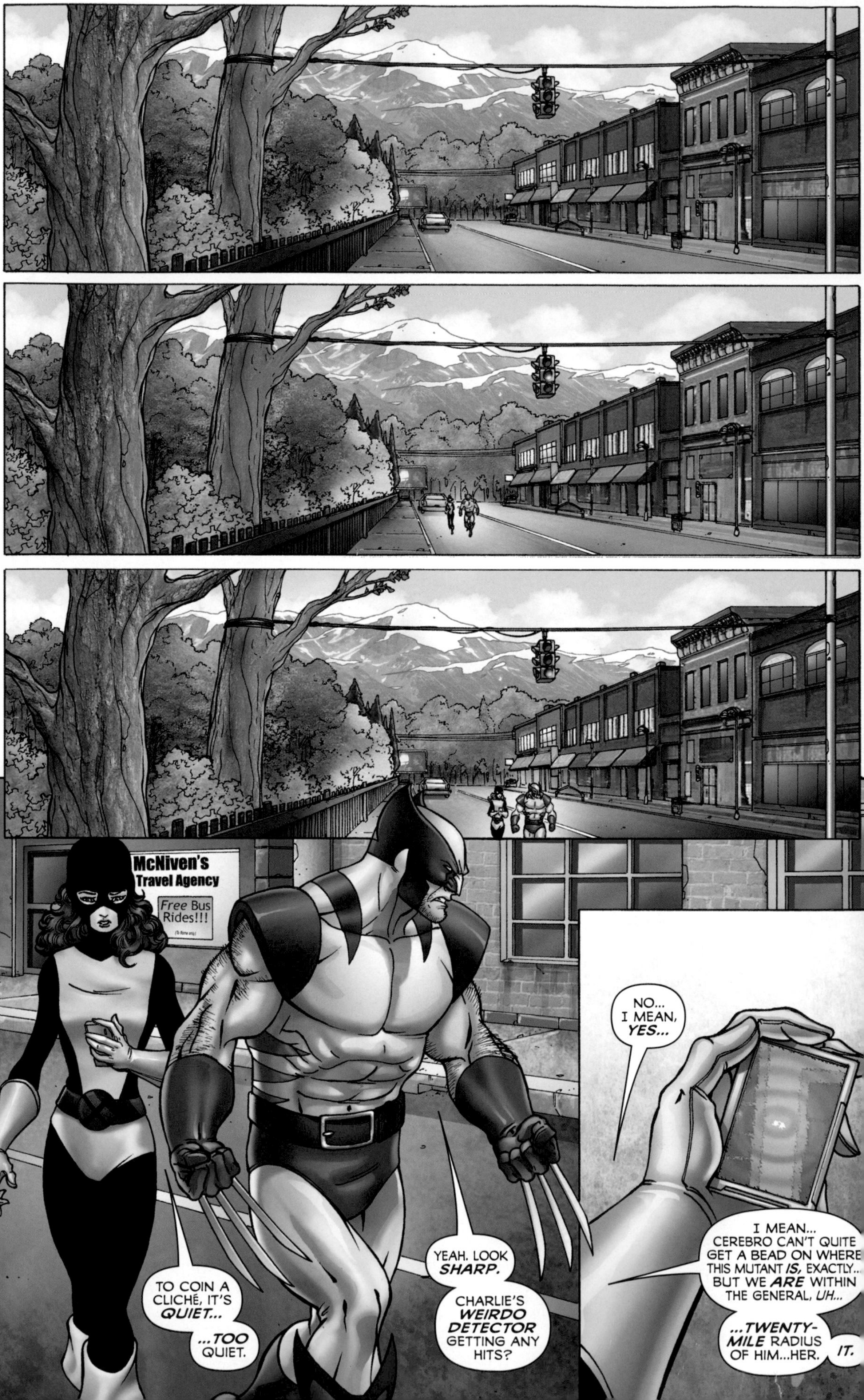

McNiven's
Travel Agency
Free Bus Rides!!!
TO COIN A CLICHÉ, IT'S *QUIET...*
...TOO QUIET.
YEAH. LOOK *SHARP.*
CHARLIE'S *WEIRDO DETECTOR* GETTING ANY HITS?
NO... I MEAN, *YES...*
I MEAN... CEREBRO CAN'T QUITE GET A BEAD ON WHERE THIS MUTANT *IS,* EXACTLY... BUT WE *ARE* WITHIN THE GENERAL, *UH...*
...TWENTY-MILE RADIUS OF HIM...HER.
IT.

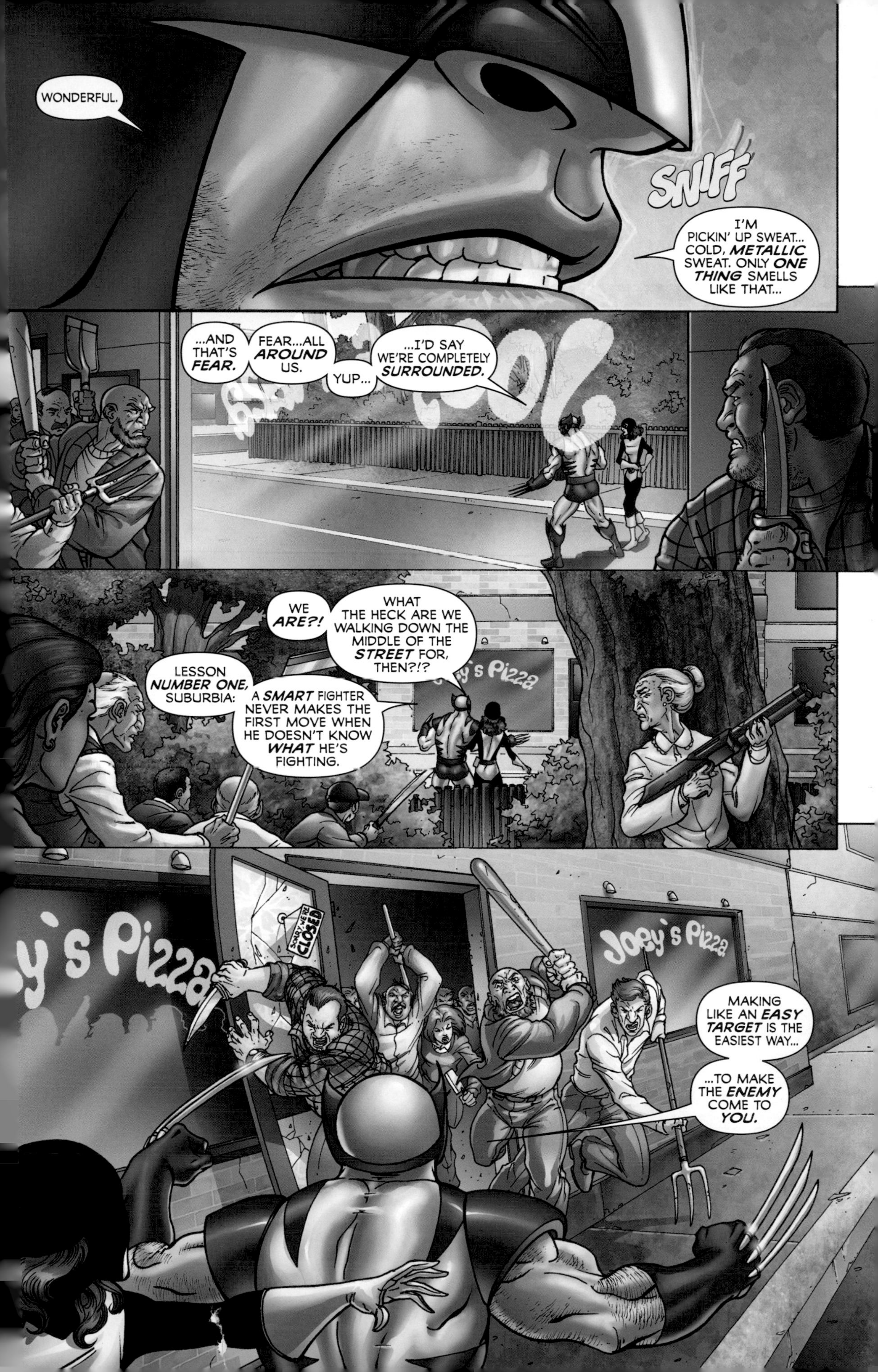
WONDERFUL.
SNIFF
I'M PICKIN' UP SWEAT... COLD, METALLIC SWEAT. ONLY ONE THING SMELLS LIKE THAT...
...AND THAT'S FEAR.
FEAR...ALL AROUND US.
YUP...
...I'D SAY WE'RE COMPLETELY SURROUNDED.
COOL
WE ARE?!
WHAT THE HECK ARE WE WALKING DOWN THE MIDDLE OF THE STREET FOR, THEN?!?
LESSON NUMBER ONE, SUBURBIA:
A SMART FIGHTER NEVER MAKES THE FIRST MOVE WHEN HE DOESN'T KNOW WHAT HE'S FIGHTING.
y's Pizza
SORRY WE'RE CLOSED
Joey's Pizza
MAKING LIKE AN EASY TARGET IS THE EASIEST WAY...
...TO MAKE THE ENEMY COME TO YOU.

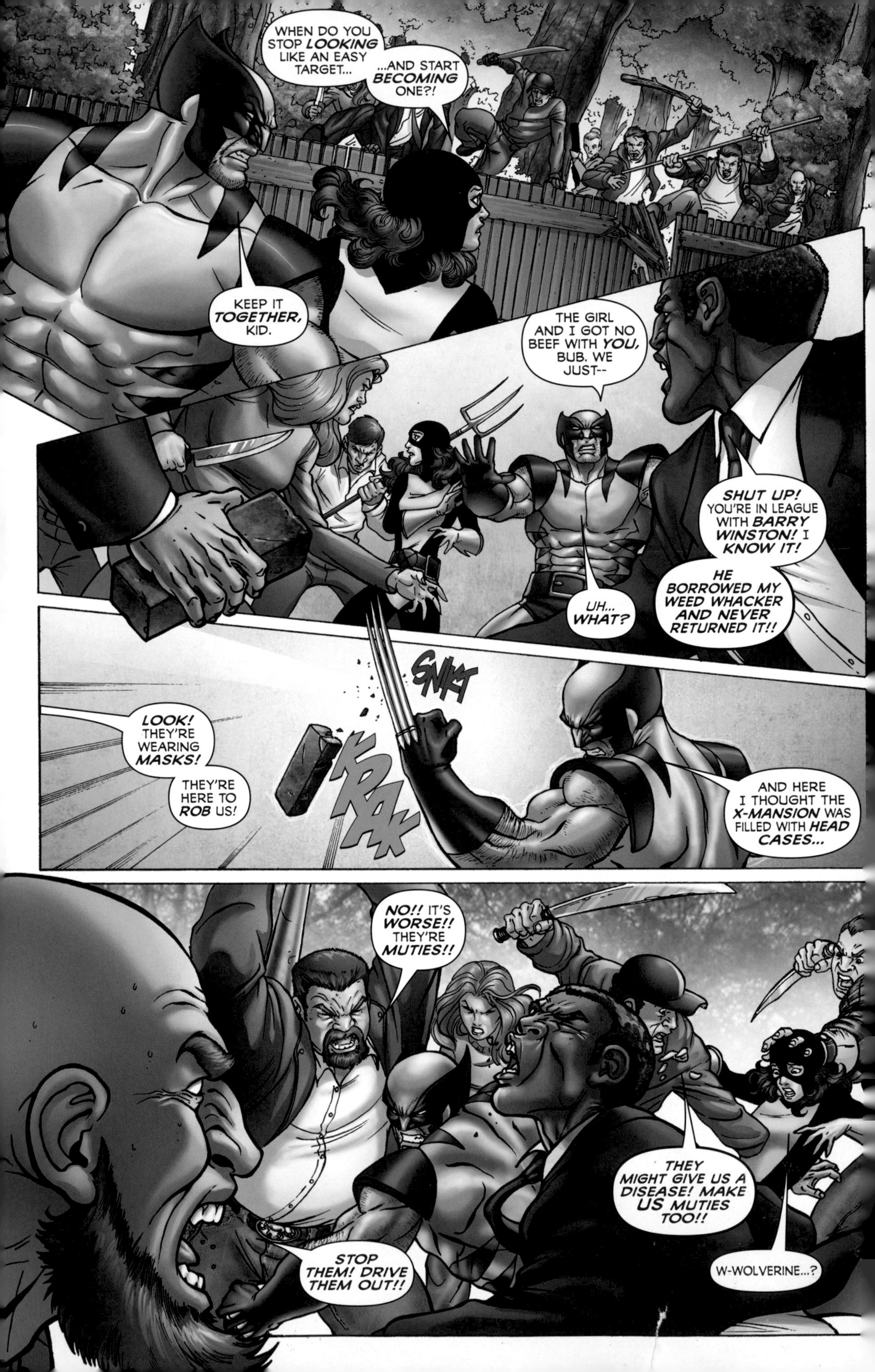

WHEN DO YOU STOP LOOKING LIKE AN EASY TARGET...
...AND START BECOMING ONE?!
KEEP IT TOGETHER, KID.
THE GIRL AND I GOT NO BEEF WITH YOU, BUB. WE JUST--
SHUT UP! YOU'RE IN LEAGUE WITH BARRY WINSTON! I KNOW IT!
HE BORROWED MY WEED WHACKER AND NEVER RETURNED IT!!
UH... WHAT?
SNIKT
KRAK
LOOK! THEY'RE WEARING MASKS!
THEY'RE HERE TO ROB US!
AND HERE I THOUGHT THE X-MANSION WAS FILLED WITH HEAD CASES...
NO!! IT'S WORSE!! THEY'RE MUTIES!!
THEY MIGHT GIVE US A DISEASE! MAKE US MUTIES TOO!!
STOP THEM! DRIVE THEM OUT!!
W-WOLVERINE...?

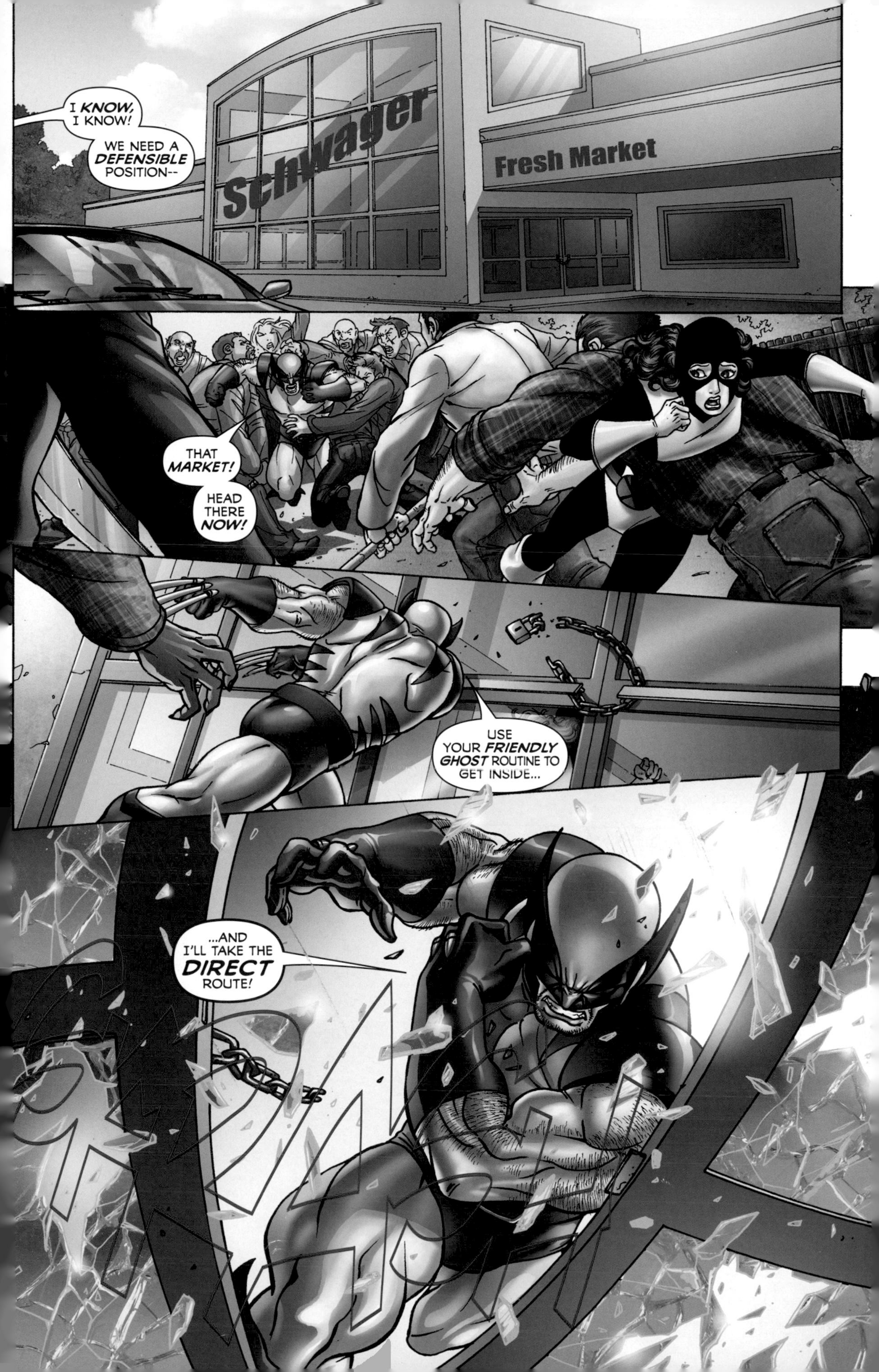
Schwager
Fresh Market
I KNOW, I KNOW!
WE NEED A DEFENSIBLE POSITION--
THAT MARKET!
HEAD THERE NOW!
USE YOUR FRIENDLY GHOST ROUTINE TO GET INSIDE...
...AND I'LL TAKE THE DIRECT ROUTE!

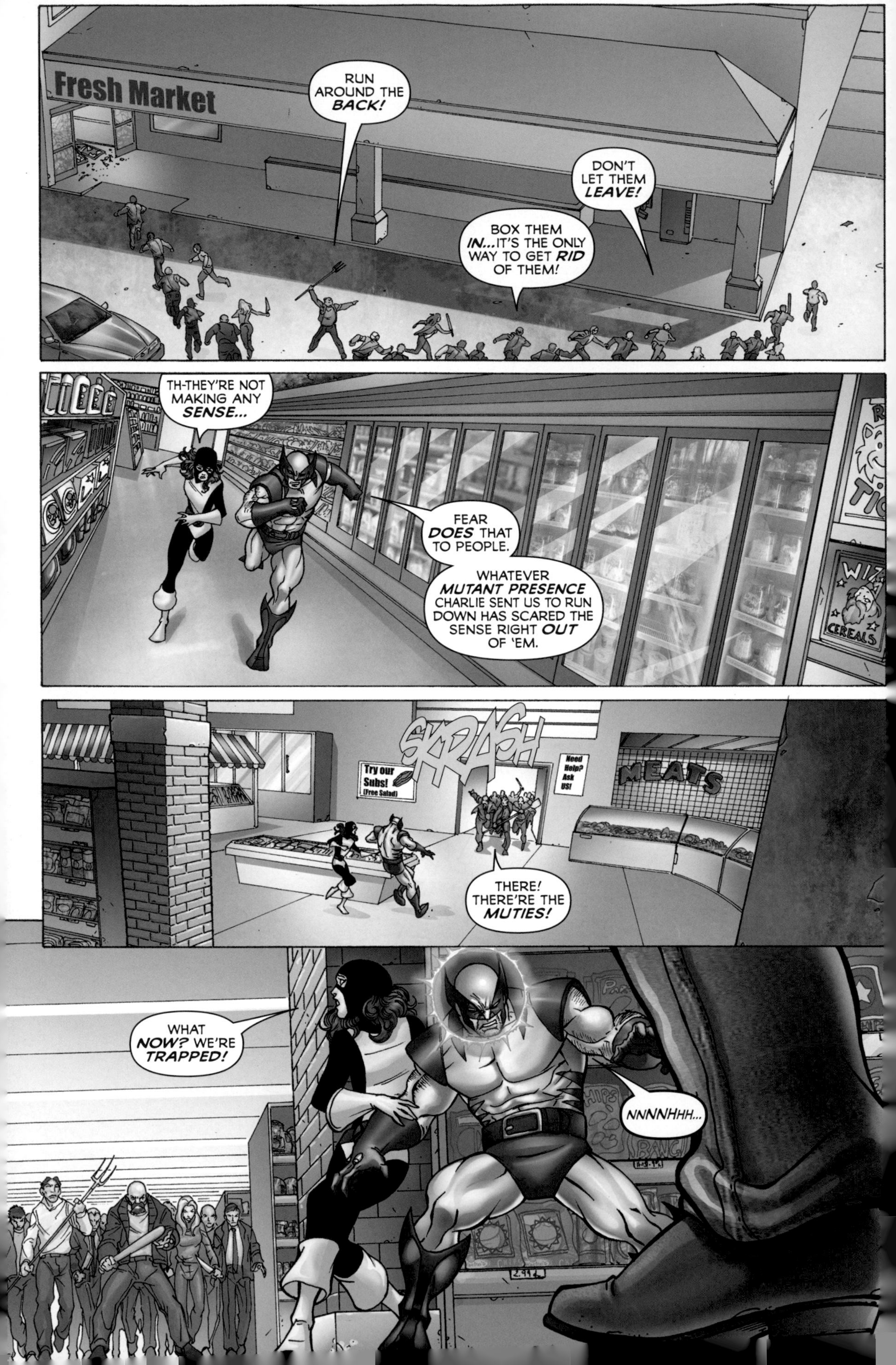
Fresh Market
RUN AROUND THE BACK!
DON'T LET THEM LEAVE!
BOX THEM IN... IT'S THE ONLY WAY TO GET RID OF THEM!
TH-THEY'RE NOT MAKING ANY SENSE...
FEAR DOES THAT TO PEOPLE.
WHATEVER MUTANT PRESENCE CHARLIE SENT US TO RUN DOWN HAS SCARED THE SENSE RIGHT OUT OF 'EM.
CEREALS
SKRASH
Try our Subs! (Free Salad)
Need Help? Ask US!
MEATS
THERE! THERE'RE THE MUTIES!
WHAT NOW? WE'RE TRAPPED!
NNNNHHH...

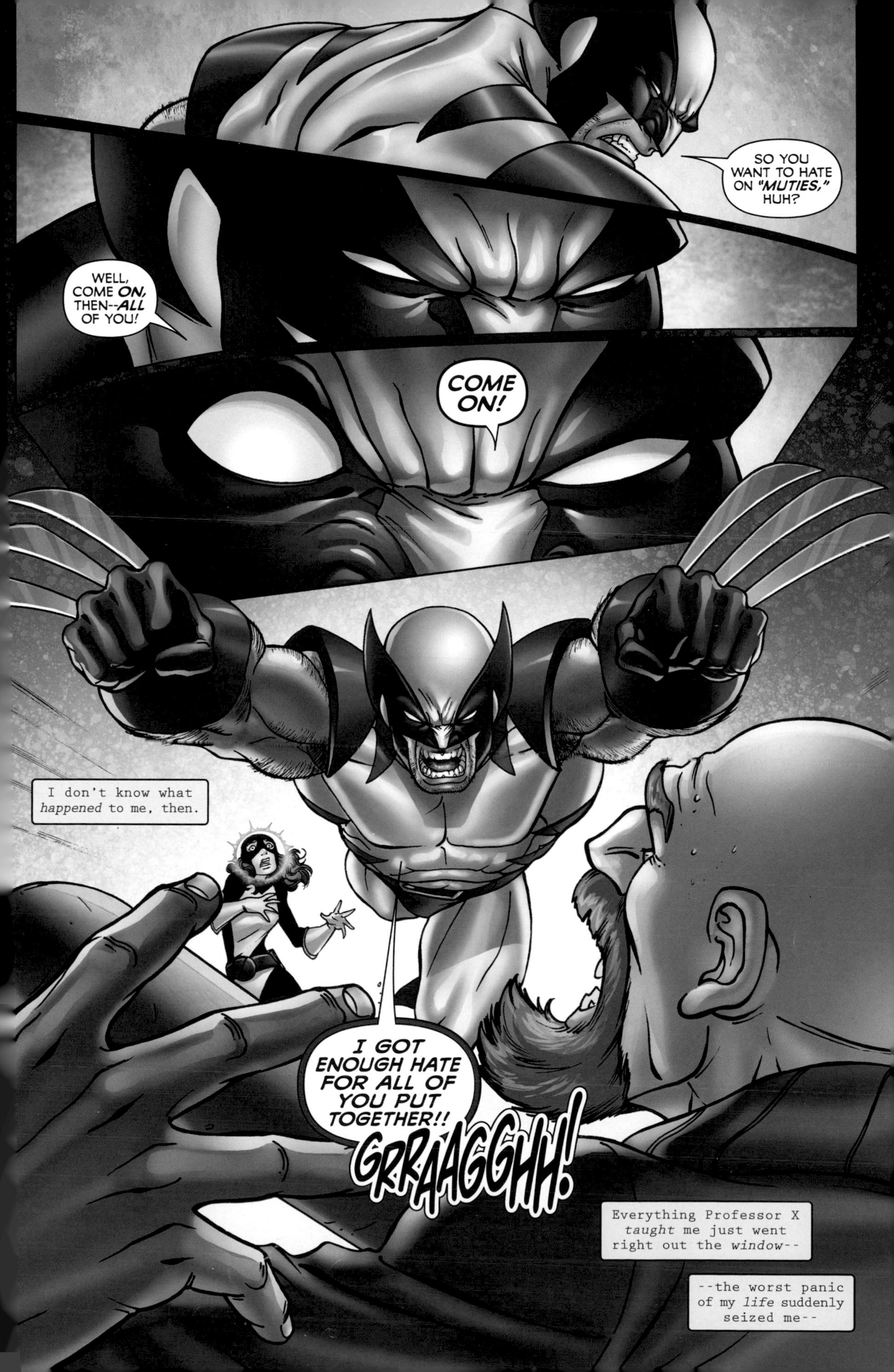
SO YOU WANT TO HATE ON "MUTIES," HUH?
WELL, COME ON, THEN--ALL OF YOU!
COME ON!
I don't know what happened to me, then.
I GOT ENOUGH HATE FOR ALL OF YOU PUT TOGETHER!!
GRRAAGGHH!
Everything Professor X taught me just went right out the window--
--the worst panic of my life suddenly seized me--

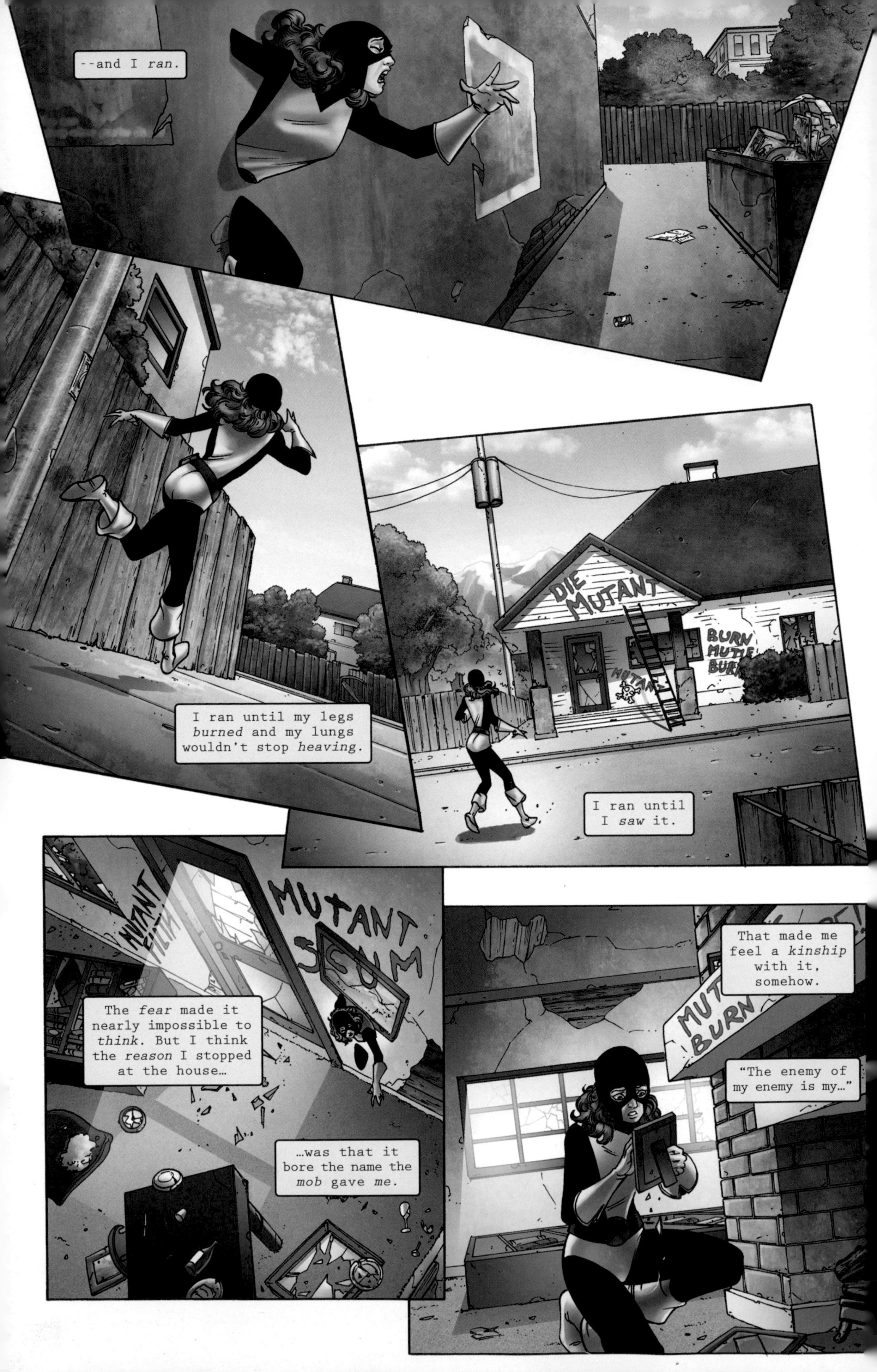

--and I *ran.*
I ran until my legs *burned* and my lungs wouldn't stop *heaving.*
DIE MUTANT
BURN MUTIE BURN
I ran until I *saw* it.
MUTANT FILTH
MUTANT SCUM
The *fear* made it nearly impossible to *think.* But I think the *reason* I stopped at the house...
...was that it bore the name the *mob* gave *me.*
That made me feel a *kinship* with it, somehow.
MUTE BURN
"The enemy of my enemy is my..."

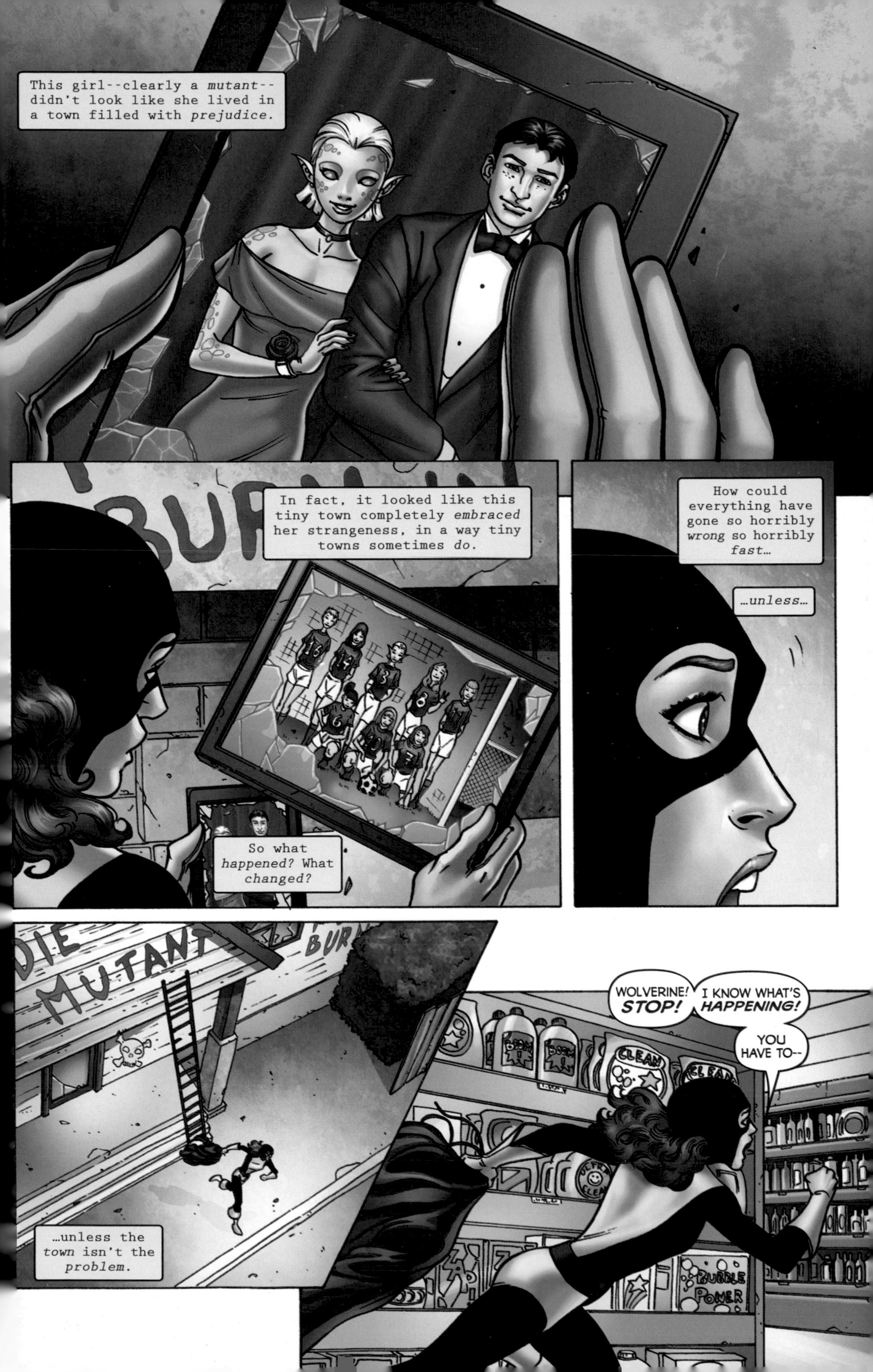

This girl--clearly a *mutant*--didn't look like she lived in a town filled with *prejudice*.
BUR
In fact, it looked like this tiny town completely *embraced* her strangeness, in a way tiny towns sometimes *do*.
So what *happened*? What *changed*?
How could everything have gone so horribly *wrong* so horribly *fast*...
...*unless*...
DIE MUTANT
BUR
...unless the *town* isn't the *problem*.
WOLVERINE! **STOP!**
I KNOW WHAT'S **HAPPENING!**
YOU HAVE TO--
CLEAN
BUBBLE POWER

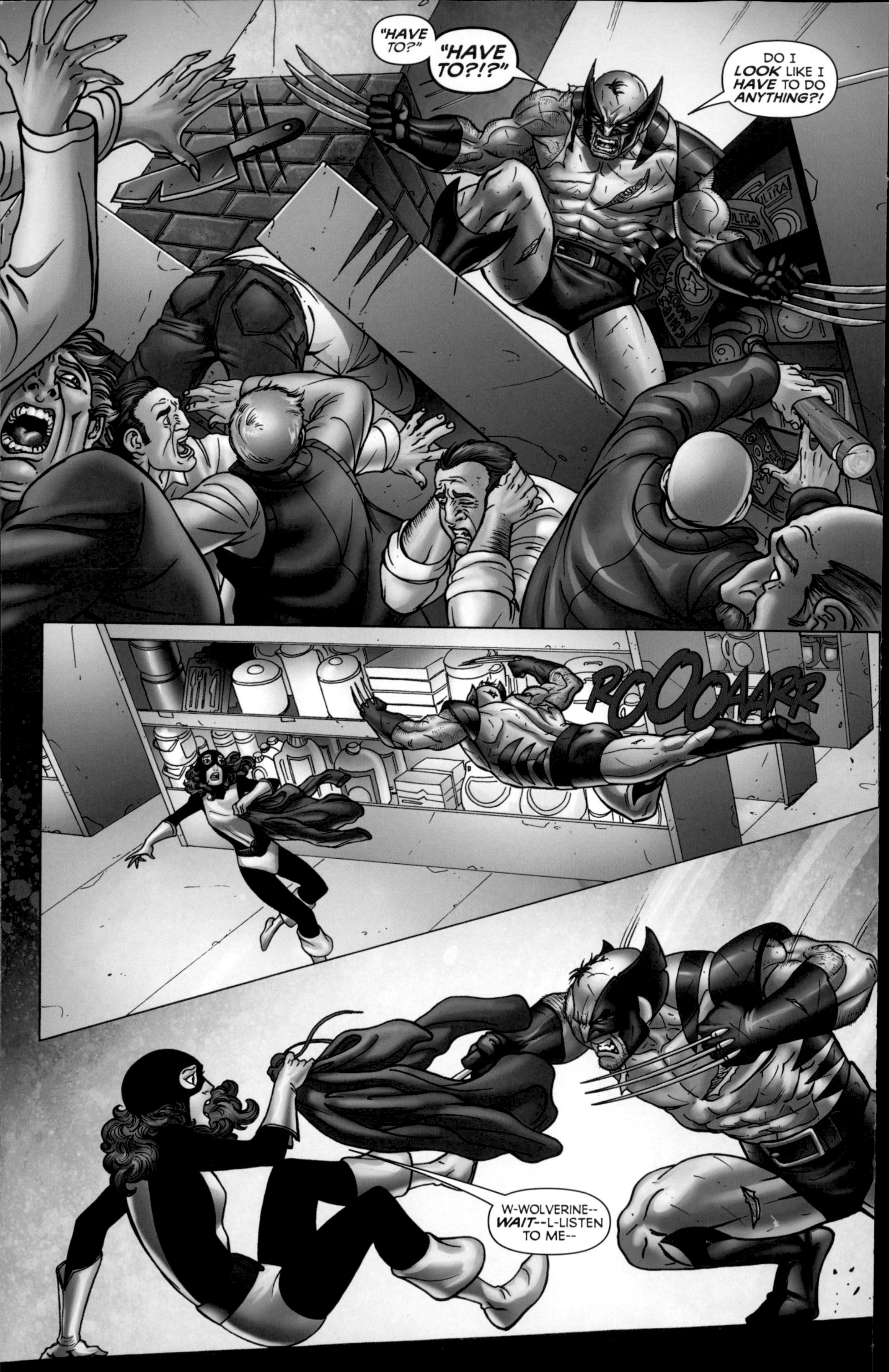
"HAVE TO?"
"HAVE TO?!?"
DO I LOOK LIKE I HAVE TO DO ANYTHING?!
ROOOAARR
W-WOLVERINE-- WAIT--L-LISTEN TO ME--

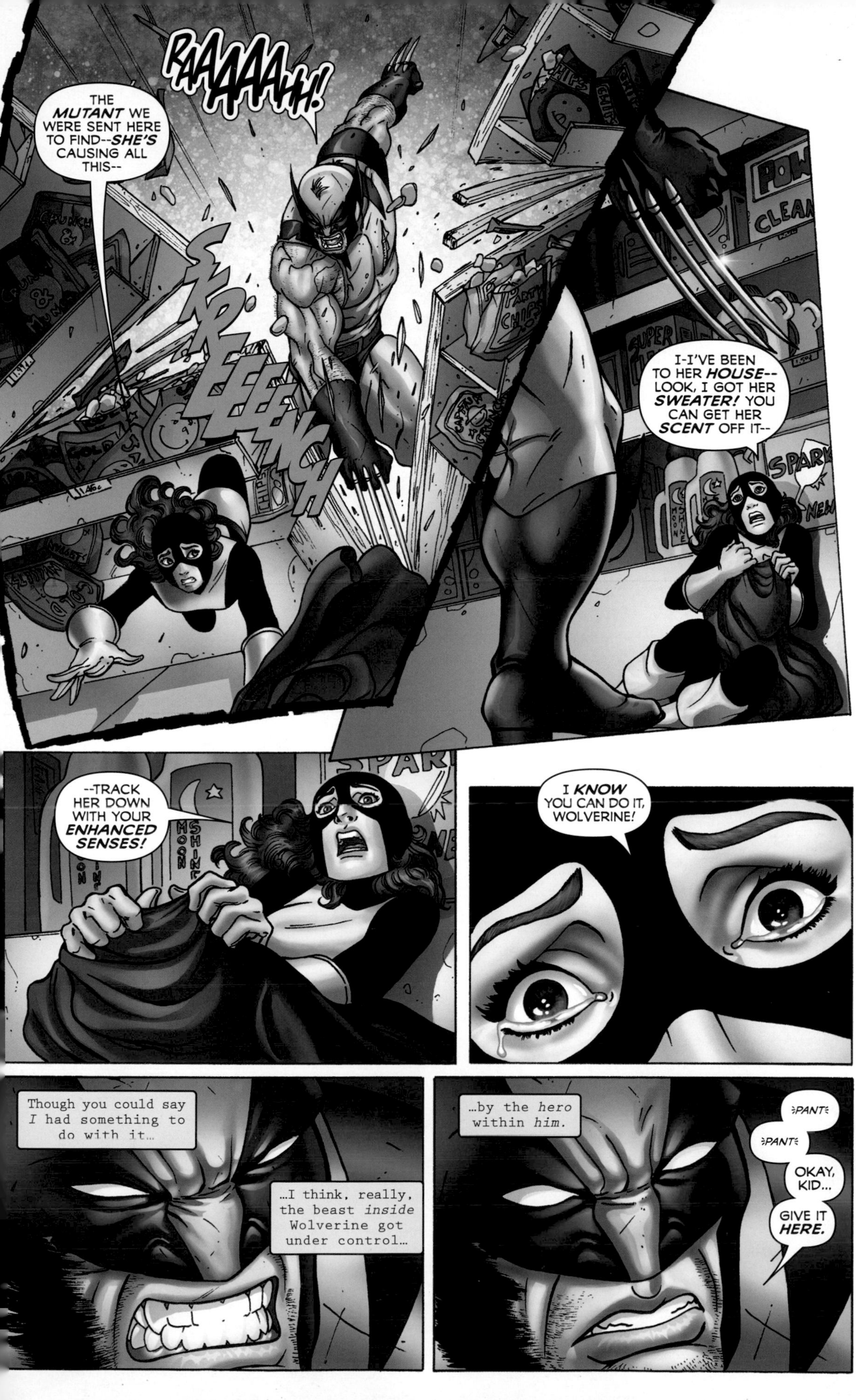

RAAAAAHH!
THE MUTANT WE WERE SENT HERE TO FIND--SHE'S CAUSING ALL THIS--
SKREEEENCH
I-I'VE BEEN TO HER HOUSE-- LOOK, I GOT HER SWEATER! YOU CAN GET HER SCENT OFF IT--
--TRACK HER DOWN WITH YOUR ENHANCED SENSES!
I KNOW YOU CAN DO IT, WOLVERINE!
Though you could say I had something to do with it...
...I think, really, the beast inside Wolverine got under control...
...by the hero within him.
PANT
PANT
OKAY, KID...
GIVE IT HERE.

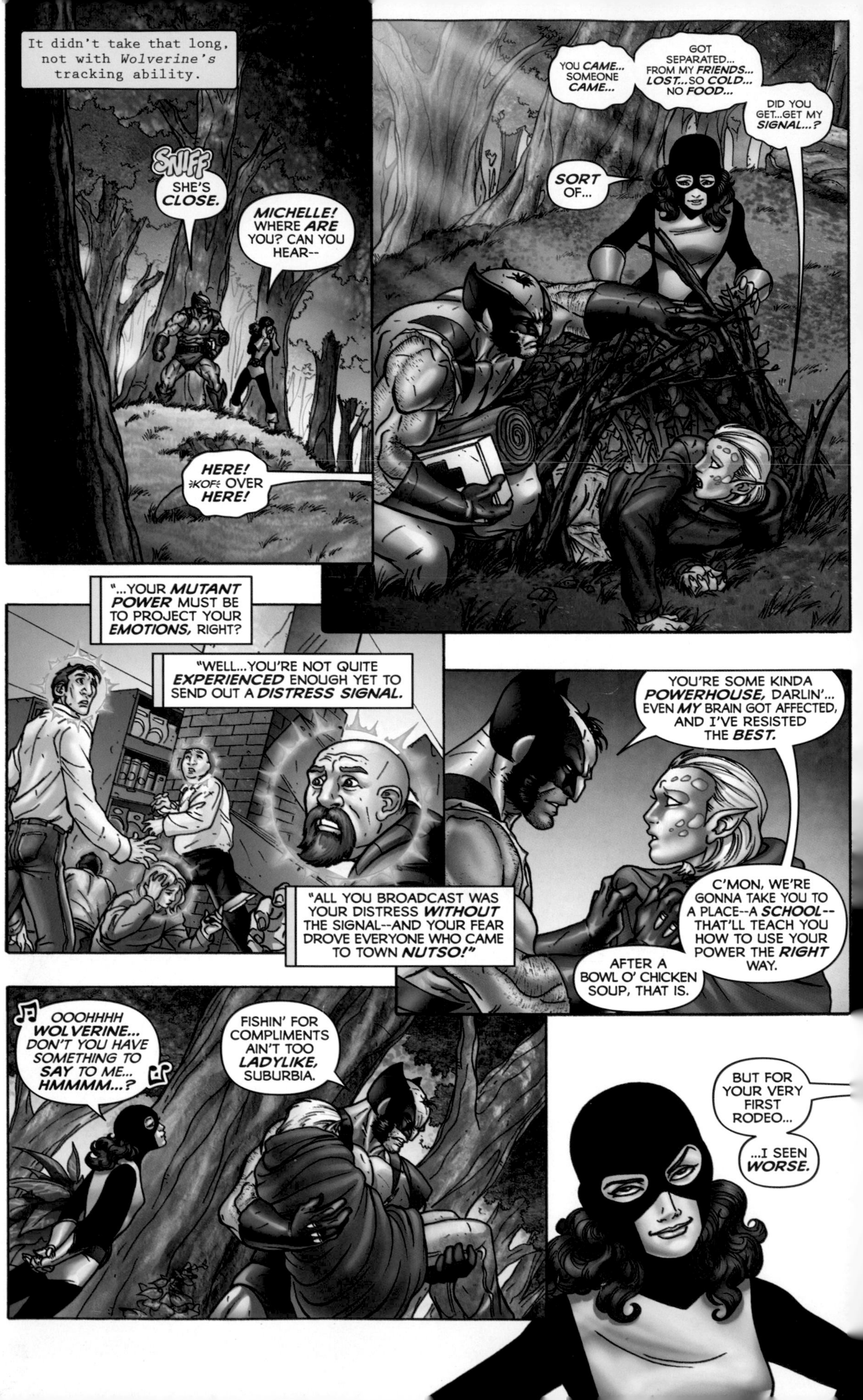
It didn't take that long, not with *Wolverine's* tracking ability.
SNIFF
SHE'S CLOSE.
MICHELLE! WHERE ARE YOU? CAN YOU HEAR--
HERE! *KOF* OVER HERE!
YOU CAME... SOMEONE CAME...
GOT SEPARATED... FROM MY FRIENDS... LOST...SO COLD... NO FOOD...
DID YOU GET...GET MY SIGNAL...?
SORT OF...
"...YOUR MUTANT POWER MUST BE TO PROJECT YOUR EMOTIONS, RIGHT?
"WELL...YOU'RE NOT QUITE EXPERIENCED ENOUGH YET TO SEND OUT A DISTRESS SIGNAL.
"ALL YOU BROADCAST WAS YOUR DISTRESS WITHOUT THE SIGNAL--AND YOUR FEAR DROVE EVERYONE WHO CAME TO TOWN NUTSO!"
YOU'RE SOME KINDA POWERHOUSE, DARLIN'... EVEN MY BRAIN GOT AFFECTED, AND I'VE RESISTED THE BEST.
C'MON, WE'RE GONNA TAKE YOU TO A PLACE--A SCHOOL--THAT'LL TEACH YOU HOW TO USE YOUR POWER THE RIGHT WAY.
AFTER A BOWL O' CHICKEN SOUP, THAT IS.
OOOHHHH WOLVERINE... DON'T YOU HAVE SOMETHING TO SAY TO ME... HMMMM...?
FISHIN' FOR COMPLIMENTS AIN'T TOO LADYLIKE, SUBURBIA.
BUT FOR YOUR VERY FIRST RODEO...
...I SEEN WORSE.

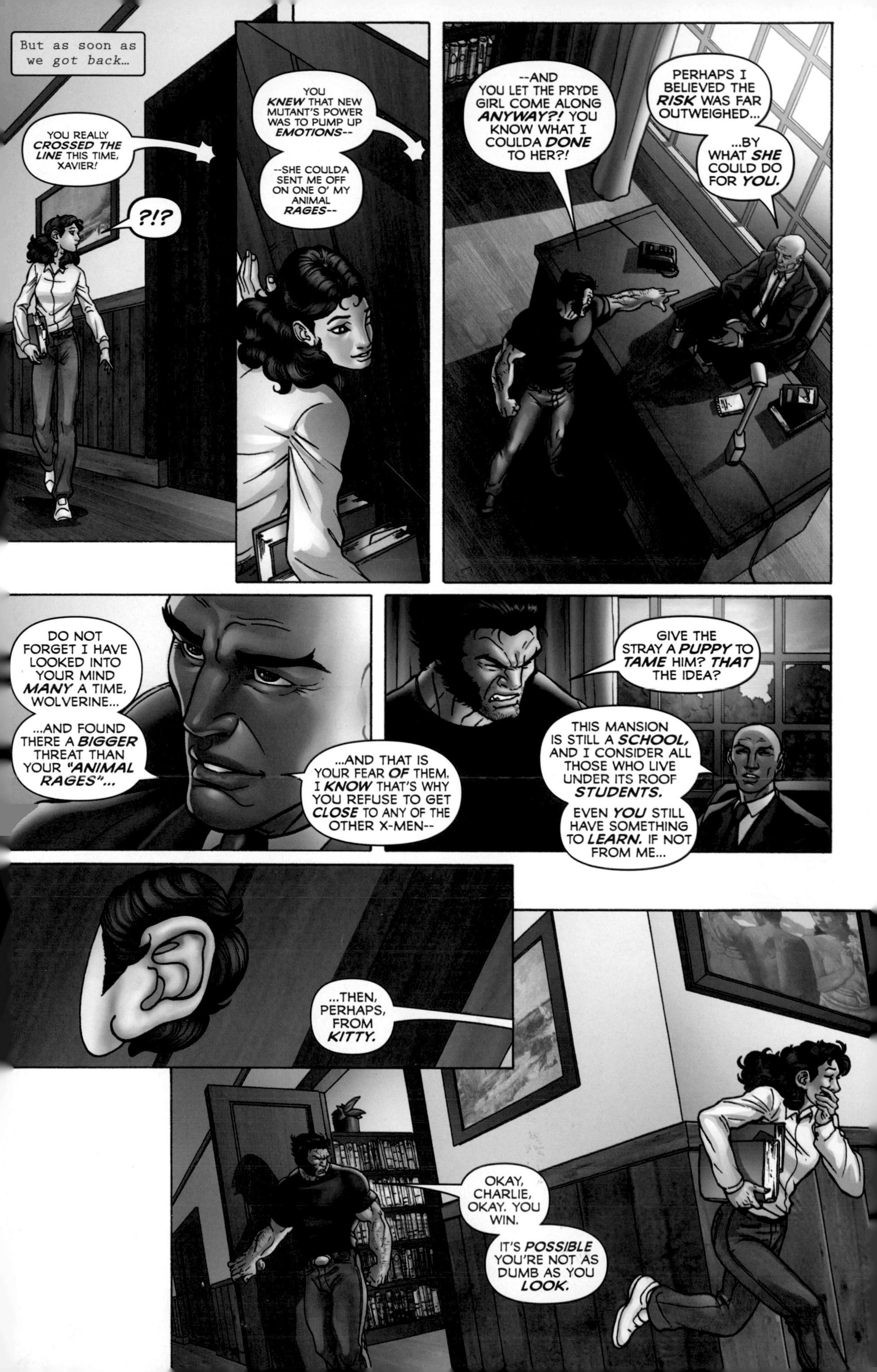

But as soon as we *got back*...
YOU REALLY ***CROSSED THE LINE*** THIS TIME, XAVIER!
?!?
YOU ***KNEW*** THAT NEW MUTANT'S POWER WAS TO PUMP UP ***EMOTIONS***--
--SHE COULDA SENT ME OFF ON ONE O' MY ANIMAL ***RAGES***--
--AND YOU LET THE PRYDE GIRL COME ALONG ***ANYWAY?!*** YOU KNOW WHAT I COULDA ***DONE*** TO HER?!
PERHAPS I BELIEVED THE ***RISK*** WAS FAR OUTWEIGHED...
...BY WHAT ***SHE*** COULD DO FOR ***YOU.***
DO NOT FORGET I HAVE LOOKED INTO YOUR MIND ***MANY*** A TIME, WOLVERINE...
...AND FOUND THERE A ***BIGGER*** THREAT THAN YOUR ***"ANIMAL RAGES"...***
...AND THAT IS YOUR FEAR ***OF*** THEM. I ***KNOW*** THAT'S WHY YOU REFUSE TO GET ***CLOSE*** TO ANY OF THE OTHER X-MEN--
GIVE THE STRAY A ***PUPPY*** TO ***TAME*** HIM? ***THAT*** THE IDEA?
THIS MANSION IS STILL A ***SCHOOL,*** AND I CONSIDER ALL THOSE WHO LIVE UNDER ITS ROOF ***STUDENTS.***
EVEN ***YOU*** STILL HAVE SOMETHING TO ***LEARN.*** IF NOT FROM ME...
...THEN, PERHAPS, FROM ***KITTY.***
OKAY, CHARLIE, OKAY. YOU WIN.
IT'S ***POSSIBLE*** YOU'RE NOT AS DUMB AS YOU ***LOOK.***

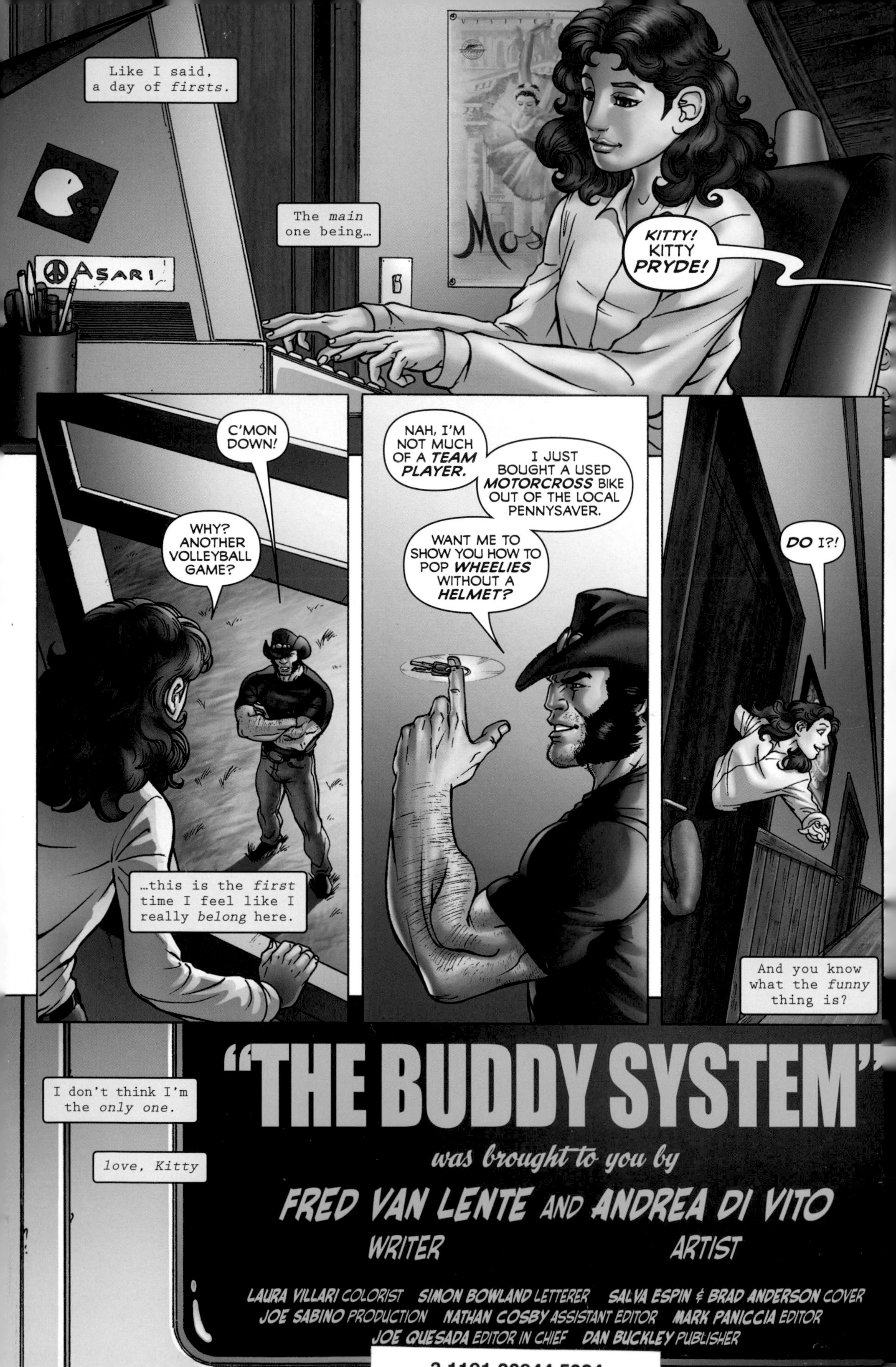
Like I said, a day of *firsts*.
The *main* one being...
ASARI
KITTY! KITTY PRYDE!
C'MON DOWN!
WHY? ANOTHER VOLLEYBALL GAME?
...this is the *first* time I feel like I really *belong* here.
NAH, I'M NOT MUCH OF A TEAM PLAYER.
I JUST BOUGHT A USED MOTORCROSS BIKE OUT OF THE LOCAL PENNYSAVER.
WANT ME TO SHOW YOU HOW TO POP WHEELIES WITHOUT A HELMET?
DO I?!
And you know what the *funny* thing is?
I don't think I'm the *only one*.
love, Kitty
"THE BUDDY SYSTEM"
was brought to you by
FRED VAN LENTE AND ANDREA DI VITO
WRITER ARTIST
LAURA VILLARI COLORIST SIMON BOWLAND LETTERER SALVA ESPIN & BRAD ANDERSON COVER
JOE SABINO PRODUCTION NATHAN COSBY ASSISTANT EDITOR MARK PANICCIA EDITOR
JOE QUESADA EDITOR IN CHIEF DAN BUCKLEY PUBLISHER